Abra Cadabra
and the Tooth Witch

Story and illustrations by
Nurit Karlin

SOMERVILLE HOUSE, USA
NEW YORK

ISBN: 1-58184-028-4
A B C D E F G H I J

Printed in Hong Kong

Originally published as *The Tooth Witch* in 1985 by J.B. Lippincott.

Somerville House, USA is distributed by
Penguin Putnam Books For Young Readers
345 Hudson Street, New York, N.Y. 10014

Published in Canada by
Somerville House Publishing,
a division of Somerville House Books Limited
3080 Yonge Street, Suite 5000
Toronto, Ontario M4N 3N1
e-mail: sombooks@goodmedia.com
Web site: www.sombooks.com

To Ariel and Asaf

$\mathcal{T}$he Tooth Witch was bored.

She worked every night.

Her job was to collect the baby teeth that children
lose as they grow older.
She would put them in her bag.
The Tooth Witch loved her work, and she
did it very well.
But after six hundred years of it,
she was getting bored.

"Every night the same old thing," she mumbled.
"It's no fun anymore," she grumbled.
She yawned.
"This bag is too heavy."

One night she dropped it.

Losing the bag of teeth was a serious matter.
The witches called a special meeting.
They decided the Tooth Witch needed a helper.

"Abra Cadabra! YOU help her!"

"ME?"

The Tooth Witch was disgusted.

"Look at you," she snorted.
"You are not a real witch.
You don't even have a broom!"

Abra Cadabra wanted to know everything about her new job.

"Why do we work at night?" she asked.
"Because witches see better in the dark," hissed
the Tooth Witch.

Another night Abra Cadabra asked,
"Don't we give the children anything in return
for the teeth we take?"
"GIVE them? Ha!" The Tooth Witch growled.
"We just take."

Abra Cadabra thought that was wrong.
She started filling her pockets with presents.
Every time she collected a tooth,
she left a surprise in its place.

One night they stopped to rest.
"The bag is almost full,"
said Abra Cadabra.
"What will we do with all these teeth?"
The Tooth Witch chortled.
"We throw them in flower beds
and they grow into rocks."

She started to laugh.

She laughed...
and laughed...
and...

Ooops!

Breaking a broom
was even more serious
than losing a bag of teeth.
The witches decided
the Tooth Witch
needed a vacation.

They sent Abra Cadabra
to bring back the bag of teeth
that was left on the moon.

On her way Abra Cadabra thought
about the teeth and the rocks.
"There must be something better to do
with all those lovely teeth."

Then she smiled.

"Of course!"

Dipping into the bag, she scattered
the teeth across the sky.

When she was done, the night
lit up with stars.
Her dress was sparkling white.
She had grown a pair of wings.
The broom had turned into a wand.

She plucked a star and put it on the wand.
She had become a fairy.
The Tooth Fairy.

And there was nothing the witches
could do about it.